A BIRTHDAY FOR BLUEBELL

The Oldest Cow in the World

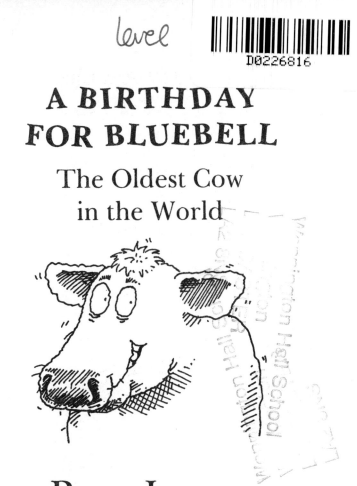

Rose Impey
Shoo Rayner

ORCHARD BOOKS

ORCHARD BOOKS
96 Leonard Street, London EC2A 4RH
Orchard Books Australia
14 Mars Road, Lane Cove, NSW 2066
First published in Great Britain 1993
First paperback publication 1993
Text © Rose Impey 1993
Illustrations © Shoo Rayner 1993
The right of Rose Impey to be identified as the author
and Shoo Rayner as the illustrator of this work has
been asserted by them in accordance with the
Copyright, Designs and Patents Act, 1988.
A CIP catalogue record for this book
is available from the British Library.
Hardback 1 85213 455 0
Paperback 1 85213 456 9
Printed in Great Britain

A BIRTHDAY
FOR BLUEBELL

Bluebell was a cow.
A very old cow.
The oldest cow in the world.
Bluebell was seventy-eight years old!

People can live to be seventy-eight.
It isn't so unusual.
But for a cow it was a record.
Bluebell was famous.
She was even on the television.

When Bluebell was seventy
she had a message from the Queen.
It said, "Well done, Bluebell."

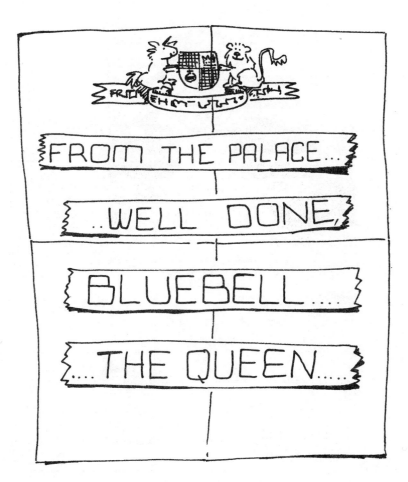

FROM THE PALACE...

..WELL DONE,

BLUEBELL...

....THE QUEEN.....

When Bluebell was seventy-one
she had a letter
from the President of America.

And a cheque for 100 dollars!

THE PRESIDENTIAL   BANK OF AMERICA

Pay Bluebell
One hundred Dollars $100-
only

The President

When she was seventy-two
Bluebell visited London
for the first time.

She went by train.
First Class!

When she was seventy-three
Bluebell flew in Concorde.
She went to visit her grandson.
He lived in Texas.

Bluebell went for a trip
in a hot air balloon
when she was seventy-four.
It was slower than Concorde,
but she liked it.

When she was seventy-five
Bluebell did a parachute jump.
She had her picture in the paper.

But her friends began to worry
that she might break her leg
or end up in hospital.
"After all," they said,
"she *is* seventy-five years old."

When she was seventy-six
her friends told Bluebell,

Bluebell was surprised.
She didn't feel old.

When Bluebell was seventy-seven
her friends gave her a television.
Then Bluebell slowed down.

She watched television all day,
every day of the week.
She never did anything else.
Her friends were sorry
they had ever given her a television.

"There is nothing else
I want now," said Bluebell.
"Nothing in the world."

So when Bluebell was seventy-eight
her friends couldn't decide
what to get her.

What can you get for a cow
who has everything?

A cow who has been everywhere.

There must be something,
they thought.
So they each tried to find out
what Bluebell would like.

Goat showed her his holiday photos.
Ski-ing in Spain.

"Do you like holidays?" he asked.
But Bluebell shook her head.

Donkey showed Bluebell his new
C.D. player.

"Would you like one?" he said.
But Bluebell shook her head.

Pig showed Bluebell tickets
for the new Adventure Fun Park.

"Would you like to go?" she said.
But Bluebell shook her head.
"It would only make me dizzy,"
she said. "I am too old for Fun Parks."

"Bluebell is so boring,"
said Hen.

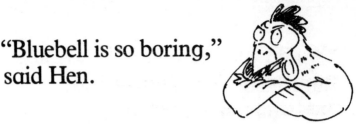

"She used to be such good fun,"
said Pig.

"It's our fault,"
said Donkey.

"It's that television,"
said Goat.

Then Hen had an idea.
"We will give Bluebell a party
for her birthday.
That will cheer her up."

"A party is a good idea,"
said Goat. "But Bluebell
has had parties before."
"Not a fancy dress party,"
said Hen.
"With party games," said Pig.
"And party music," said Donkey.
"And no television!" said Goat.

For the next week
the animals were busy
making their plans.
They didn't tell Bluebell.
They wanted it to be a surprise.

Every day Bluebell watched television,
as usual.
No one came round to visit.
No one asked her to go out
for a walk
or a swim.
Bluebell began to feel lonely.

"A television is nice," she said,
"but not as nice as friends."

Bluebell went out
to look for her friends.
But her friends were too busy.

"Sorry, Bluebell, just going out,"
said Goat.

"No time to stop," said Pig.

"Too much to do," said Donkey.

"See you later," said Hen.

Bluebell went home
feeling very sorry for herself.
"Nobody wants me any more,"
she said. "Now I am old."

On Saturday morning
Bluebell got out of bed.
She didn't turn on her television.
She just sat in her chair
feeling miserable.

But then the postman came.
He brought her lots of cards.
They made her smile.

33

Hen knocked at the door.
She was holding a large box.
"Happy Birthday, Bluebell,"
she said.
"You look funny," said Bluebell.
"What is in that box?"
"Open it and see," said Hen.

COSTUME
HIRE Co.

It was a fancy dress outfit.
"I can't wear that," said Bluebell.
"I am too old to dress up."
"Nonsense," said Hen.
"You are as old as you feel.
Come on, put it on.
Everyone will be here soon."

When the other animals arrived
Bluebell was dressed
and ready for the party.
"Happy Birthday, Bluebell,"
said Donkey
and Pig
and Goat.

Bluebell couldn't stop laughing.
"You all look silly," she said.
"So do you," said Hen.
"Who cares," said Goat.
"Time for the games," said Pig.

First they played
'Pin the tail on the donkey'.
"Be careful," said Donkey.

Then they played
'Apple Bobbing'

and 'Musical Bumps'

and 'Pass the Parcel'.

The other animals let Bluebell win.
After all, it was her birthday.

Next Donkey put on some music
and all the animals danced.
Everyone danced with Bluebell
because it was her birthday.

And then they had the party food.
Hen had cooked it all.
She had made a cake too.

There were seventy-eight candles.
Bluebell tried to blow them out.
She was soon out of breath.
The other animals had to help her.

"You are not as fit
as you were," said Hen.
"Too much television," said Goat.
"Tomorrow we will go for a walk,"
said Pig.
"And a swim," said Donkey.

"Yes," said Hen.
"We have to get you fit
if you are going to live
to be a hundred."

"Well," said Bluebell,
"next year I think I might try
wind-surfing. I have always
wanted to try wind-surfing."
"Why not," said the other
animals. "After all,
you *are* only seventy-eight."

What do you get if you cross a cow with a bird?
Cheep milk!
What do you get if you cross a cow and a sheep and a goat?
The Milky BAA Kid!
What do you get if you sit under a cow?
A pat on the head!

Other great **ANIMAL CRACKERS**

A BIRTHDAY FOR BLUEBELL

HOT DOG HARRIS

TINY TIM

TOO MANY BABIES

A FORTUNE FOR YO-YO

SLEEPY SAMMY

PHEW, SIDNEY!

PRECIOUS POTTER

WE WANT WILLIAM!

RHODE ISLAND ROY

WELCOME HOME, BARNEY

PIPE DOWN, PRUDLE!